An Elm Tree and Three Sisters

by Norma Sommerdorf ✳ illustrated by Erika Weihs

Viking

VIKING
Published by the Penguin Group
Penguin Putnam Books for Young Readers,
345 Hudson Street, New York, New York 10014, U.S.A.
Penguin Books Ltd, 27 Wrights Lane, London W8 5TZ, England
Penguin Books Australia Ltd, Ringwood, Victoria, Australia
Penguin Books Canada Ltd, 10 Alcorn Avenue, Toronto, Ontario, Canada M4V 3B2
Penguin Books (N.Z.) Ltd, 182-190 Wairau Road, Auckland 10, New Zealand

Penguin Books Ltd, Registered Offices: Harmondsworth, Middlesex, England

First published in 2001 by Viking,
a division of Penguin Putnam Books for Young Readers.

10 9 8 7 6 5 4 2 1

LIBRARY OF CONGRESS CATALOGING-IN-PUBLICATION DATA
Sommerdorf, Norma.
An elm tree and three sisters / by Norma Sommerdorf; illustrated by Erika Weihs.
    p.   cm.
Summary: When three young sisters plant a tiny elm tree in their barren back yard,
they find it becomes an integral part of their lives as they grow older.
ISBN 0-670-89308-0
[1. Sisters—Fiction. 2. Trees—Fiction.] I. Weihs, Erika, ill. II. Title.
PZ7.S6968 El 2000 [E]—dc21 99-050919

Printed in Hong Kong
Set in OptiWorcester-Round
Book design by Teresa Kietlinski

The illustrations were created with oil paints on acid-free gesso-coated boards.

To the Anderson cousins now
and for generations to come
　　　　—N. S.

Dedicated to those who plant a
tree and make the world a better
place for all of us
　　　　—E. W.

This is the tale of an elm tree
and three sisters,
and this is the beginning of it.

A tiny elm tree grew along a small stream
running through a farmer's field.
The tree could have lived a whole life there,
but that was not to be.

There were three sisters
named Mary, Mabel, and Molly
who lived with their father and mother
in a small town surrounded by farms.

Mary, the oldest one, had a serious look
and a thick brown braid down her back.

Mabel, the middle one, had wide gray eyes
and long hair that shone like a copper kettle.

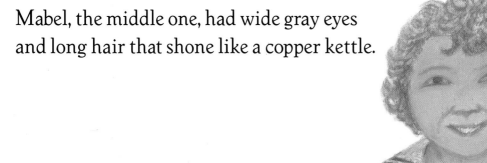

Molly, the youngest one, had blonde curls
and a mischievous grin.

From their bedroom window they saw the sun come up
where the railroad tracks touched the horizon.
Standing on the front steps
they could see the grain elevators reaching to the sky.
From the porch, they saw the sun set
behind tall cornstalks in the field.

In back of the house, the wide, flat yard stretched
all the way to the barn on the edge of the pasture.

Mary, Mabel, and Molly stared at the big, empty yard.
Mabel said, "What this place needs is a tree."
Her sisters agreed.

"Let's ask if we can take the horse and wagon
and look for a tree," Mary said.

They hitched up a horse and wagon while Father watched.
Mary held the reins tightly as Mabel and Molly
waved good-bye.

They drove a long way and could not find the right tree.
One was too big to take home.
One was in somebody's yard.
One was just too small.
At last, they went down by a little creek.

Many trees grew there—
poplars and box elders and willows and elms.
By the creek the ground was soft.
Mary was careful not to get the wagon stuck.

Her sisters jumped out and ran from tree to tree.
"Come see this one," Mabel called out.
"I'd pick that one," said Mary,
pointing to one near the wagon.
"I think this one is just perfect," said Molly, putting her
hand around one near the water.
At last the three sisters agreed on the tiny elm tree.

They were careful as they dug around the roots
and lifted it into the wagon.
The green leaves waved in the breeze as the wagon
wheels bounced over the bumpy road.

At home, they dug a hole between the house and the
barn, right in the middle of the barren yard.
Together they lifted the tree out of the wagon
and planted it firmly.
Each girl filled a bucket with water to pour around it.

The tree looked much smaller than it had down by the creek,
but they were proud they had a tree of their very own.

As the sisters walked to school during the snowy winter, they passed the tiny tree bent by stormy winds.

In spring, the tree began to sprout new leaves,
and they were happy it had lived through the cold weather.

During the next years, the tree grew slowly and steadily.
Mary, Mabel, and Molly helped their mother and father
plant gardens, milk cows, and feed chickens.

Sometimes they ate a picnic lunch by the tree.
Molly looked up through the leaves on the young branches.
"Whenever will this tree be big enough
to hold a swing?" she asked.

The sisters measured the tops of their heads
against the trunk of the tree.
"We're growing faster than the tree," said Mabel.

The spring Mary finished school
the tree was big enough to have a swing.
Father helped the girls put it up.

That fall Mary left to teach
in a country school not far from home.
She coiled her long braid into a bun,
laughed, and said, "I'm not too old to swing."
She soared as high as the swing could go.

A few years later, Mabel was married in the cool, dark parlor.
The guests kissed the bride with the copper-colored hair
and stayed for wedding cake served under the tree.

Four years later the tree was larger,
and Molly was married outside under its shade.
When the wedding was over, she wrapped her arms
around its wide trunk.
"Thank you for a beautiful place for a wedding," she said.

Years went by, and the sisters often came back home.
Sometimes their relatives came
for a family reunion on the lawn.
Tables were set up beneath the spreading elm tree.
Its thick trunk held branches to shelter all of them.
Molly's children played with Mabel's children.
Mary pushed her nieces and nephews in the swing.

Many years passed.
Mary began to teach in the town school.
She lived in her own little house on the edge
of the yard, shaded by the elm tree.
Mabel became a widow
and moved to a small house near the cornfield.

The day came when Father and Mother were buried
in the cemetery across the railroad tracks.
Molly moved back to live in their big white house
because she was all alone now, too.

The three sisters lived near each other again.
Between the houses was their own great elm tree.
The branches arched toward each of their houses.
They welcomed its shade at afternoon coffee time.

One summer Molly noticed dead leaves on the tree
and discovered two withered branches.
An inspector came by and tied an orange ribbon
around the trunk.
"This old beauty has a disease," he said.
"It has to come down, or the disease will spread
to other trees."

Together the sisters watched
as the work crew cut off the biggest branches.
They flinched as they heard the sound of the saw.
They remembered the day they brought the tree
from the creek and planted it
in the middle of the empty yard.
"Good old tree, it didn't get to live a whole life," said Mary.
"Our tree saw some very happy times," said Molly.

One spring day Molly's three great-granddaughters
came for a visit.
They led Mary, Mabel, and Molly outside to sit
in lawn chairs on the grass.
"We brought you a present," the little girls whispered.
"Cover your eyes and don't peek."

When Mary, Mabel, and Molly opened their eyes
they saw a tiny new tree.
When the tree was firmly planted,
the girls held hands
and danced around it.

Mary, Mabel, and Molly looked back
on their many years.
"We've seen many good days," they agreed,
"but this is one of the best."

This is the tale of an elm tree
and three sisters,
and this is the beginning of it.

For Reed and Sadie. —L. A.

To all the people that I loved, love, and will love. —S. S.

STERLING CHILDREN'S BOOKS
New York

An Imprint of Sterling Publishing Co., Inc.
1166 Avenue of the Americas
New York, NY 10036

ISBN 978-1-4549-1904-9

Distributed in Canada by Sterling Publishing Co., Inc.
c/o Canadian Manda Group, 664 Annette Street
Toronto, Ontario, Canada M6S 2C8
Distributed in the United Kingdom by GMC Distribution Services
Castle Place, 166 High Street, Lewes, East Sussex, England BN7 1XU
Distributed in Australia by NewSouth Books
45 Beach Street, Coogee, NSW 2034, Australia

For information about custom editions, special sales, and premium and corporate purchases,
please contact Sterling Special Sales at 800-805-5489 or specialsales@sterlingpublishing.com.

Manufactured in China
Lot #:
2 4 6 8 10 9 7 5 3 1
03/17

www.sterlingpublishing.com

The illustrations were created digitally.
Design by Irene Vandervoort

Ella WHO?

BY

Linda Ashman

ILLUSTRATED BY

Sara Sanchez

STERLING CHILDREN'S BOOKS

New York

The movers left the doors wide open.
That's probably how she got in.

They were lugging furniture and stacking boxes—LOTS of boxes.
That's probably why no one noticed her.

Plus, she's a *smallish* elephant.
And she was standing behind all those potted plants.

I told Mom right away.

"There's an elephant in the living room."

"*Ella* WHO?"

"An elephant," I repeated. "In the living room."

"Oh, *Ella*! From next door, right?" she said.
"So glad you're making friends!"

I grabbed some cookies. Good thing, because the
elephant was hungry.

"Let's go upstairs," I said. "You can help me unpack."

I told my dad, of course.

"I'm taking the elephant to my room."

"Ella WHO?"

Then Charlie started wailing.

"Will you and Ella please check on the baby?"

Charlie looked *very* happy to see us.
The elephant rocked his cradle and hummed softly.

Charlie went right back to sleep.

"Shhhh," I whispered. "Don't wake him."
I didn't need to worry. Elephants are very
light on their feet. (Surprising, I know!)

The elephant helped me unpack.

Then we played
dress-up,

had a tea party,

and read some of
our favorite books.

But I could tell she wanted to go outside.

The elephant was *not* very good at hide and seek.

She was a little *too* good at wiffle ball.

And the seesaw was a problem.

But we both liked the pool. I sprayed her with the hose.
She sprayed me. We were soaked!

Vroom!

I ran inside for towels.
Grandma was cleaning up after the movers.

"How'd you get so wet?" she shouted over the
roar of the vacuum.

"The elephant sprayed me."

"Ella WHO?" she asked. "Oh, never
mind. Just don't track in mud."

We were setting up the tent
when a man rang the doorbell.

"I'm looking for a baby elephant," he said.
"Someone reported seeing one in the neighborhood."

"An elephant?!" exclaimed Mom.

"I think we would have noticed an elephant," said Dad.

"Do you have a description?" asked Grandma.
"We'll keep an eye out."

The man left some flyers, took a last look around,
and drove away.

MISSING!
Fiona the Elephant

Description:
Large ears
Big feet
Long proboscis
Grayish complexion
A tad wrinkly
Loves apples
Dislikes green beans

If found, please call
555-2546.

The description *did* seem to fit her.
Still, maybe it was a *different* missing elephant.
There was only one way to be sure.
I grabbed some apples and green beans.

"Fiona?" I asked.
She nodded.

I called the number on the flyer.

It was sad to say *goodbye*. Fiona was my first new friend!

But I knew she missed her mother.

The truck showed up right away.
I gave Fiona some apples for the road.

We hugged goodbye,

for Fiona

then waved to each other until
the truck turned the corner.

Inside the house, everyone was relaxing after the busy day.
"There you are!" said Mom. "We were just looking for you."
"I was saying goodbye to the elephant," I said.
"Ella WHO?" asked Dad.
"You know, the girl next door," said Mom. "She's very nice."

I hope Fiona visits again soon.
Luckily our neighborhood has
lots of interesting wildlife.